Pictures
Ingrid Godon

Words
Toon Tellegen

I WISH

Translated from the Dutch by
David Colmer

Copyright © Toon Tellegen, 2011

Copyright © Ingrid Godon, 2011

Originally published in the Dutch as *Ik wou* by
Lannoo Publishers: www.lannoo.com.

English language translation © David Colmer,
2020

First Elsewhere Edition, 2020

Library of Congress Cataloging-in-Publication
data is available upon request

Elsewhere Editions
232 3rd Street #A111
Brooklyn, NY 11215
www.elsewhereeditions.org
Distributed by Penguin Random House
www.penguinrandomhouse.com

Previous versions of several of these translations
first appeared in *Modern Poetry in Translation
No. 2, 2015*

This book was published with the support of
Flanders Literature (www.flandersliterature.be).

This book was made possible by the New York State
Council on the Arts with the support of Governor
Andrew M. Cuomo and the New York State
Legislature.

Archipelago Books also gratefully acknowledges
the generous support from Lannan Foundation,
Nimick Forbesway Foundation, the Carl Lesnor
Foundation, the National Endowment for the Arts,
the New York City Department of Cultural Affairs,
and Dutch Foundation for Literature/Nederlands
Letterenfonds.

FLANDERS LITERATURE

NEW YORK STATE OF OPPORTUNITY. | Council on the Arts

ART WORKS. | National Endowment for the Arts | arts.gov

NYCulture CITY OF NEW YORK

Nederlands letterenfonds dutch foundation for literature

PRINTED IN ITALY

I wish

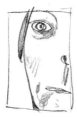

INGRID GODON is a born observer. She carefully reads eyes, faces, and postures, recording them all in her art. Inspired by the Flemish Primitives, the great Italian Renaissance painters, and the photographer Norbert Ghisoland, she depicts restrained emotions and poignant vulnerabilities. Ingrid Godon's evocative drawings are charged with great seriousness and strangeness, with immense compassion for ordinary people. Ingrid Godon was awarded the Boekenpauw Award and the Gouden Griffel in 2001 for her book *Wachten op Matroos*. She also won the Boekenpauw Award in 2015 for *Ik denk*. She was nominated three times for the ALMA Award and was named in the 2016 IBBY Honour List.

In his short poems, TOON TELLEGEN sought out stories behind Ingrid's many faces. In masterful, poetic pieces he renders their most intimate thoughts and desires. One child says, "I wish I had more courage… Ordinary courage. Not heroism or recklessness. Everyday courage." Tellegen's reveries and streams of thought lend wondrous words to the fears, anger, desires, and wistful surprise in the portraits' eyes. Toon Tellegen received the Theo Thijssen Prize in 1997, the Constantijn Huygens Prize in 2007, and he was a finalist for the Hans Christian Andersen Award in 2006.

DAVID COLMER's translations from the Dutch stretch across a wide range of genres including literary fiction, nonfiction, children's books, and poetry. He has won a number of awards including the Biennial NSW Premier and PEN Translation Prize for his body of work in 2009. Together, he and writer Gerbrand Bakker won the 2010 International IMPAC Dublin Literary Award and the 2014 Independent Foreign Fiction Prize for the novels *The Twin* and *Ten White Geese* respectively. In 2014, Colmer was also shortlisted for the PEN Award for Poetry in Translation for *Even Now*, a selection of the poetry of Hugo Claus.

I wish

I wish

there were pictures everywhere of two arms sticking up in the air

with a red diagonal stripe through them and

DESPAIRERS WILL BE PROSECUTED

written underneath.
If someone despaired anyway, they'd get arrested
and thrown into jail.
I don't like despair.
They'd have special police to take care of it:
"Ah, I see, desperate… at the end of your
tether… you're coming with me!"
If I ever got desperate again – it could happen –
I'd make sure nobody saw me.
I'd wait until it was dark and I was in bed
under the covers,
convinced nothing would ever come right again
between me and everyone else.

THIS IS my last request.

When I die, I want them to check

how long someone's still thinking of me.

There'll be a machine they can use.

There isn't one yet. But when I die there will be.

Mark my words.

A memoriammaphone.

After one year, ten days, six hours and nineteen

minutes: *tring-tring, tring-tring.*

Nobody's thinking of me anymore.

I'm forgotten forever. Deleted is what they'll call it.

And if someone thinks of me again later by mistake, just for a moment,

maybe because they looked at a photo and somebody pointed me out

and asked, "Who's that?" and somebody else racked their brains

and managed to remember that it's me, that won't count anymore.

Once you're gone, you're gone.

ALICE

I BELIEVE in God, but I can prove he doesn't exist.

Everyone believes me: "Yes, you're right, he doesn't exist…

That argument is watertight…

How could we have been so wrong…"

Then I have God all to myself.

At night in bed, when I tell him what I've done that day,

he gets angry and wants to leave me.

I am a complete disappointment to him.

He thrashes about under the blankets

like a fish out of water.

"You don't have anywhere to go…" I say.

"Nobody else believes in you…"

After a while he stops thrashing about.

Just like a fish out of water.

Often I feel sorry for him and whisper,

"Poor God…"

"You can say that again," he mumbles.

After that I fall asleep.

I don't know what he does.

OSCAR

IF I ever saw an ad like this:

> "Wanted: secretive boy
> for secret duties"

I would apply.
"At last, at last!" they would exclaim when I
walked in because they'd never seen anyone
as secretive as me.
I exceeded all expectations because I wasn't
just secretive, I was inscrutable too.
True inscrutability is a rare thing.
The next day I would start on my secret
duties, concerning which I am not at liberty
to make any statements.
At night I'd go to bed with Band-Aids over my mouth
to make sure I didn't give anything away in my sleep.
And if someone asked, "What are you doing these days?"
I'd shrug my shoulders and reply,
with an inscrutable expression on my face,
"Nothing special."
If only they knew!

LEONARD

I WISH I wasn't scared of dying.

There are people who aren't scared of death.

When they see him coming they just stand there

calmly and call out, "Hey, Death!

It's so nice to see you!"

But those same people hide in the basement during

thunderstorms or scream and climb up on tables

when they see a mouse.

I like mice and thunderstorms.

Maybe everyone needs to be scared of something,

it doesn't matter what, just like everyone needs

to breathe and eat and drink.

Otherwise you die.

I WISH I always had an alibi.

    If they arrested me, I'd smile and say,

    "I am sorry to disappoint you,

    but it couldn't possibly have been me.

    This is my alibi."

    I'd pull it out and smack it down

    on the table in front of them.

    If they thought it wasn't enough, I'd have another.

    I'd be the boy with a thousand alibis.

    They'd sigh and open the door of the station

    and let me go again.

    In the clear no matter what,

    and I'd be like that forever!

MARCEL

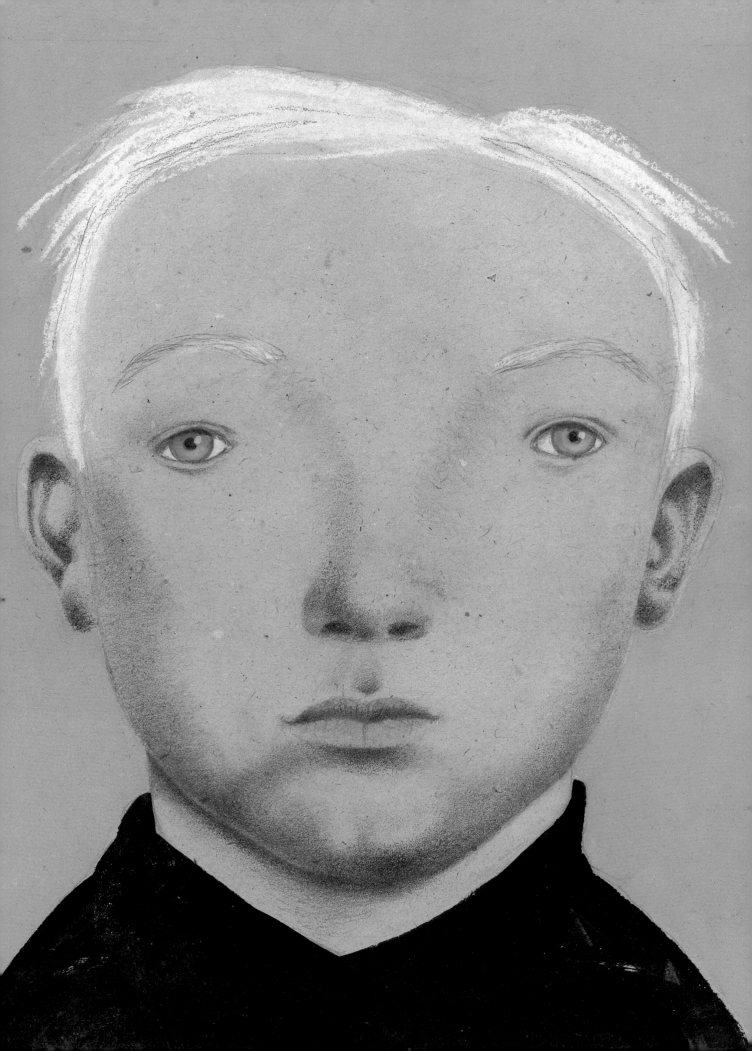

I WISH I never had to blush.

I hate blushing.

If blushing was a worm, I'd stomp on it right away.

And if it was a person, I'd report them to the police.

Blushing is criminal.

Blushing is cowardly, always sneaking up on you.

It grabs me from behind and lifts me up

until everyone can see my face.

"She's blushing! Oh, look how pretty she is when she blushes!"

There should be posters

stuck up everywhere saying

WANTED DEAD OR ALIVE: BLUSHING

and under that a list

of its crimes against me.

Blushing is war on my face.

I wish

I wish

I was walking past a wall one day.

It would be spring and the sun would be shining

and suddenly I would see my name.

That's me!

Under my name it says that dot-dot-dot loves me

and will never love anyone else. Oh, dear, dear, dear…

(and then my name again)

There's a heart with an arrow through it too, with her name

at the bottom on the left and mine on the right at the top.

Dot-dot-dot is a girl at school, who if you ask me has never

once so much as looked in my direction.

I wish I'd walk past a wall like that one day.

I WISH that a boy would wake up tomorrow morning,

get up, get dressed, pull on his coat, go outside

and start to run, not understanding why he's running,

but still going faster and faster, past streets, canals

and squares, around a corner, up some steps.

I wish he couldn't slow down

and would run straight through a front door,

and through another door into a room.

Until he came to a halt just in front of me.

I'm in the room. I've just gotten up.

I wish he would then look at me, smile at me,

wrap his arms around me and whisper

in my ear that he now, finally, understands

what he's living for.

And that—when he's done all that for me—

I would then whisper back that now I,

for the very first time, understand it too.

OLGA

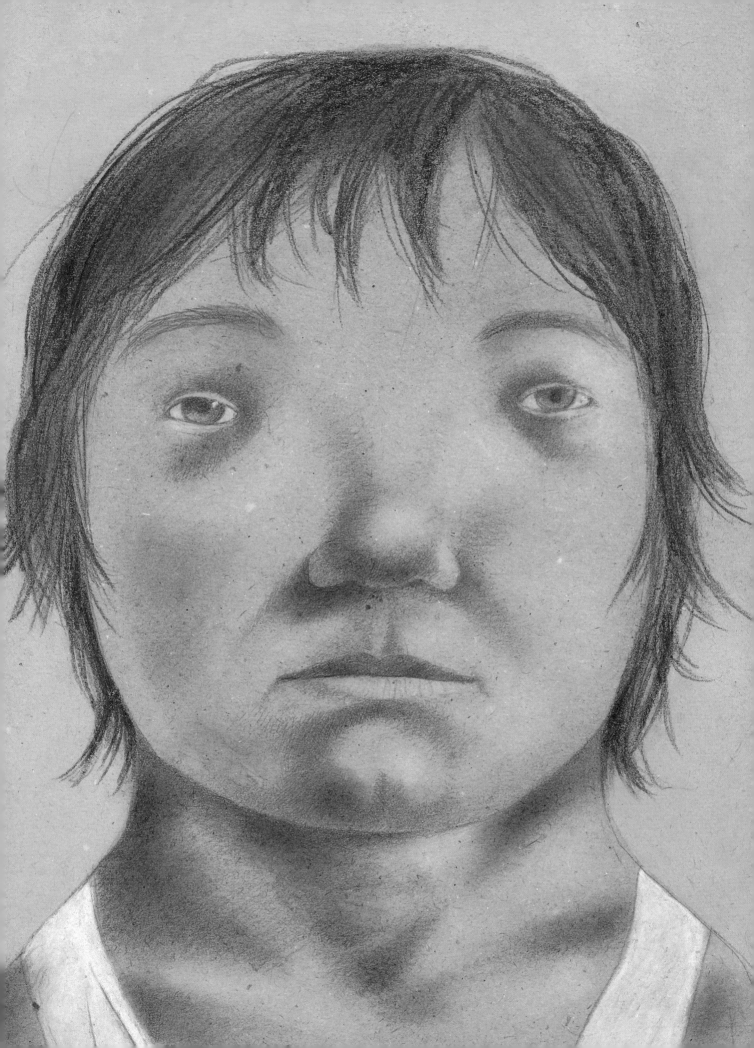

I WISH I had more courage.

I've got so little of it...

If courage was something you could buy,

I'd spend all my money on it.

It would be my most valuable possession.

Ordinary courage. Not heroism or recklessness.

Everyday courage.

People would talk about me like this:

"See that kid there?"

"Yes."

"Do you know what he is?"

"No."

"Brave. Very brave."

"Really?"

"Yes, really."

Then I'd get happiness too at no extra cost.

ANTON

I WISH I'd go to school and

find that a miracle had happened.

I'd turn the corner just in time

to see my school slowly coming

loose from the ground.

All the teachers would be hanging out the windows,

shouting, "Help! Help!"

Behind them I'd see aliens with cauliflowers

on their shoulders instead of heads.

They'd scratch the blackboards with their fingernails.

One alien would stand on the roof and scream,

"Nkrgostahowplogtsk." Or something like that.

Nobody knew the language of aliens and nobody

knew where they were going either or what they

were planning to do with the teachers.

The school would disappear into the clouds. The shouts

of the teachers and the scratching on the boards would die out.

Where the school had been there'd be a field and

we'd start a game of soccer.

It wouldn't be like we had anything else to do.

CLEMENT

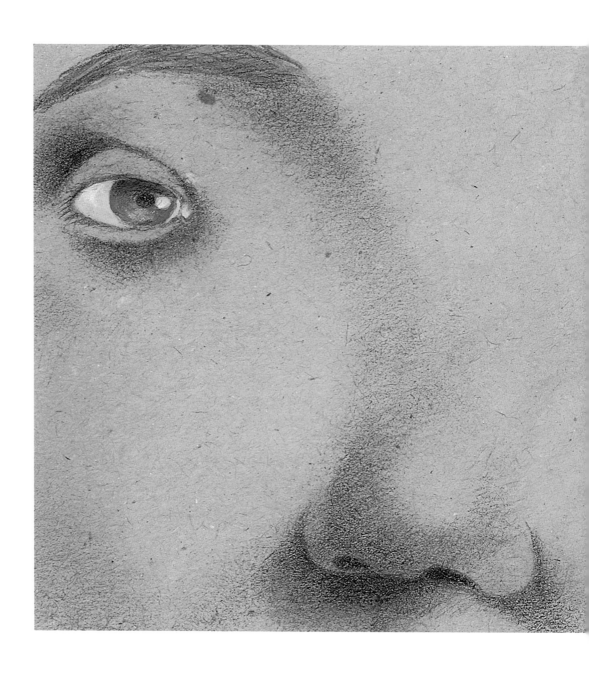

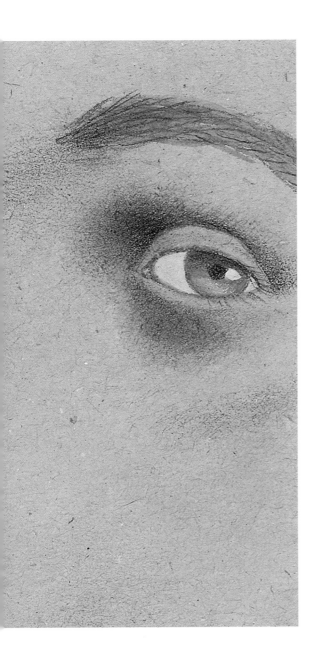

"THAT, I WILL NOT DO."

If I could one day say those words.

A crowd. On a square.

Men in uniform. Snipers

on the rooftops.

A menacing silence. Perhaps a sobbing child.

"Shhh! Shhh!"

An order. Cutting.

Everyone holds their breath,

guns are cocked.

Then I step forward.

In a quiet but clear voice,

easily understood, I say,

"That, I will not do."

On behalf of everyone.

JOSÉ

IF I think about it, it's actually pretty weird

that I'm me.

Couldn't I just as easily have been someone else?

Or something else?

If I'm in a forest looking at ants crawling in all directions,

I often think, that ant, there, that could have been me.

And then I follow one with my eyes and imagine

that I'm it and really busy and have to keep going

with a little straw that's way too big in my jaws

and there's an enormous creature looming over me,

staring at me and blocking out my sun.

Imagine if I was that ant! But then who'd be me?

The ant?

It's best not to think about things like that.

There are so many things it's best not to think about.

Maybe more than what you can think about.

JULIA

40

WHEN I'M sad I always think: and the saddest

is yet to come… Then, besides being sad,

I'm scared too.

Why do I do that?

When I'm happy I never think:

and the happiest is yet to come…

When I'm happy, I'm always just happy.

All it takes is for a girl to smile at me

and I'm there.

The saddest doesn't exist: that's what I should think!

And the happiest does.

REMI

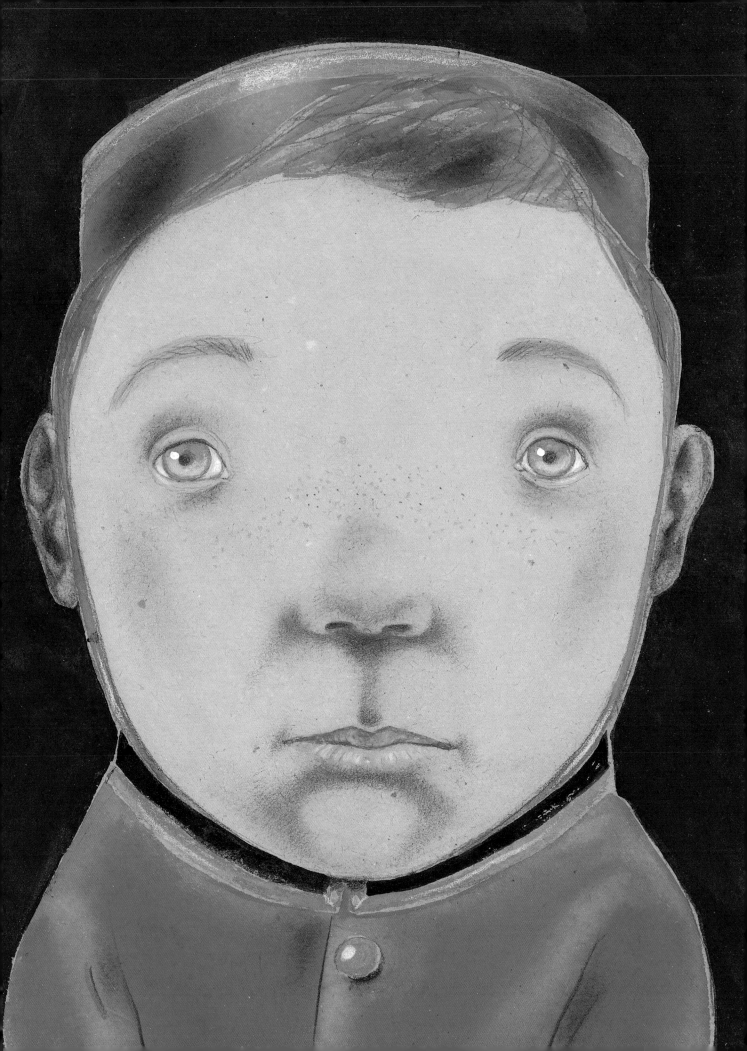

I wish

I wish

I had a wand with a mysterious, retroactive power

I could use on people I hated.

After I'd touched them, they wouldn't exist anymore.

Nobody had ever heard of them.

They had never existed.

I wouldn't hate them anymore. Because how

can you hate somebody who has never existed?

But still, I think I'd have a feeling that something

was wrong. Without being able to work out what it was.

Maybe it's a leftover from a forgotten hatred of somebody

I touched with my wand.

Like the hull of a ship that got hit by a torpedo

and sank to the bottom of the ocean.

I don't know.

WHENEVER something terrible happens, I immediately

think: it's my fault.

Crimes, attacks, accidents.

Maybe I said something wrong to someone, who got so

upset they said something much, much worse to someone else,

who passed it on to somebody, who screamed it at someone,

who ran away, jumping out of a window and landing

on top of someone who had just bought a China vase,

which they now dropped and broke, and that made them so

angry they thought, I've had enough… and fired a rocket

that started a war.

I'm to blame for that war.

Not earthquakes, floods, and volcanic eruptions,

I can't help them.

When things like that happen, I let out a secret

sigh of relief. Sometimes I even feel like

cheering (though I don't).

PAOLO

I WOULD LIKE first of all to express my sincere thanks

to whoever gave me my looks.

I mean: IN-sincere.

Because I look horrible.

When I look in the mirror, I always think:

you are so ugly...

Girls walk past me with their faces turned.

If I looked different, they'd jostle around me instead,

all shouting at once:

"He's mine!"

"No, mine!"

"Mine!"

"Mine!"

Then I'd make a calm and well-considered choice

while the other boys grumbled and rode off on their

scooters with nobody to sit on the back.

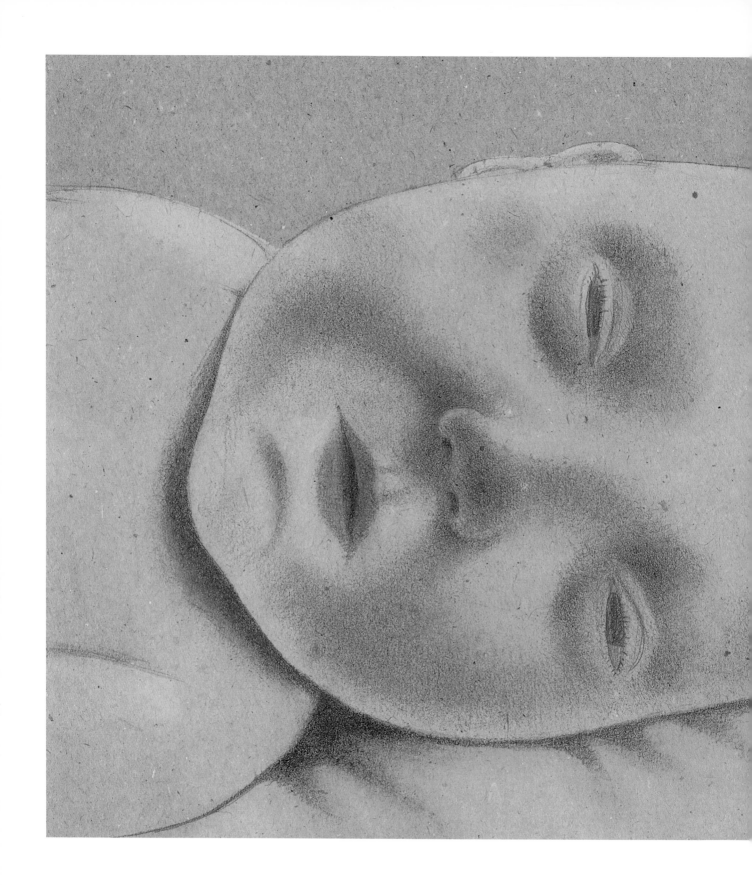

52

TITUS

I WISH happiness was a thing and I

     found it somewhere and took it home with me.

     I wouldn't tell anyone I'd found it.

     I'd hide it and only get it out

     when I was sure I was completely alone.

     Then I'd buff it up.

     Happiness needs to shine, even if it's secret.

     If I felt down and nothing I wanted was working out,

     if everyone hated me and I was in the hospital with two

     broken legs, boils, toothache, conjunctivitis,

     chicken pox, and scarlet fever, I could tell

     myself: but I still have my happiness,

     it's still there where I put it!

CARL

I HAVE a little list of conditions I have to

      fulfill to be satisfied with myself.

      When I read that list, I think,

      there are two things I can do:

      either make a list that's even shorter

      or never be satisfied with myself.

      What should I do?

I WISH I was music, a song that everyone was singing,

whistling, humming. One everyone had

on their mind when they were in love.

I wish everyone would hear me now and then,

somewhere unexpected, stop what they were doing,

close their eyes and listen until I was finished,

then sigh deeply and carry on.

But I'd never be completely finished.

Never forever.

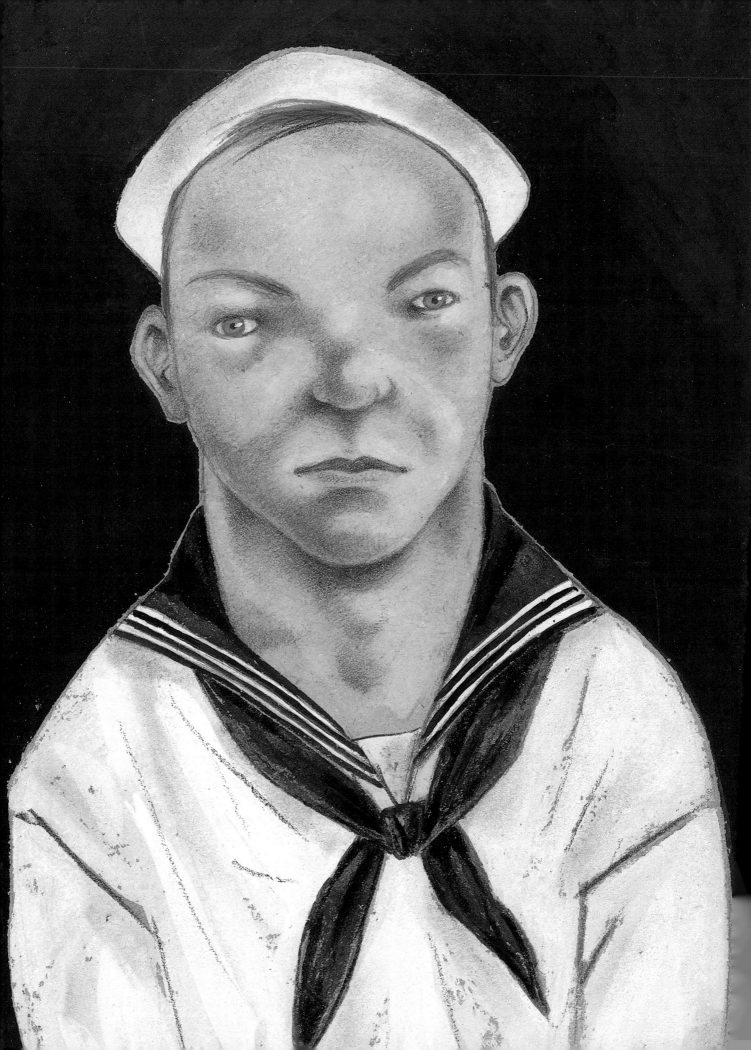

I WISH I didn't know what everyone knows.

  What does everyone know?

  That everyone dies in the end.

  That's the only thing everyone knows for sure.

  But not me—I wouldn't know that.

  I'd be the only one in the world who didn't know.

MARIE
& ROSE

I wish

I wish

I could just shrug myself off

and when I thought about myself the next thought would always be:

haven't you got anything better to think about?

There is always something better to think about.

There are so many questions nobody knows the answer to.

I wish I couldn't care less about myself, that if I happened

to bump into myself I'd nod at most, but not say anything.

That way I'd be free to go my own way. Undisturbed.

I want to think. But not about myself.

I WISH something had suddenly been canceled, without

anyone knowing why, and I'd climbed up onto a table

after I'd heard and was dancing with joy.

"It's off! It's off!" I would

call out quietly while dancing.

It would be the happiest I'd been in my whole life!

I wish I had that feeling every day.

Without anyone being able to tell by looking at me.

RED RIDING HOOD

I WISH I was alone.

    No, that would still be too much.

    I wish I was nobody.

    That I was sitting here in this room and somebody

    came in, looked around and said,

    "No, he's not here. There's nobody here."

    I wish I was still somebody for just one person,

    who came in a little later

    and closed the door behind her.

I WISH I had a friend and we'd both

    saved each other's lives at risk of our own.

    Out of the sea, one of us. Out of a burning house, the other.

    We had already lost consciousness.

    And although we lived on opposite sides of the world,

    we would always stay each other's best friend.

    That's the kind of friend I'm looking for.

    But setting my house on fire or going too far out to sea

    and hoping someone happens to come sailing past

    is too risky.

    And I don't know if afterwards I'd be brave enough

    to rescue them from a burning house or a raging sea.

JEAN

I WISH I could say yes.

     The sun is shining and someone asks

     if I'm coming to the beach.

     I'd love to go to the beach,

     but I say no.

     Somebody else wants to play soccer.

     No.

     To the movies.

     No.

     Somebody else again asks

     if we can be friends.

     No.

     Are we enemies then?

     No.

     I'm really good at writing yes.

     Yes. Yes, of course. Yes, sure. Oh, yes!

     But saying yes, that's too hard.

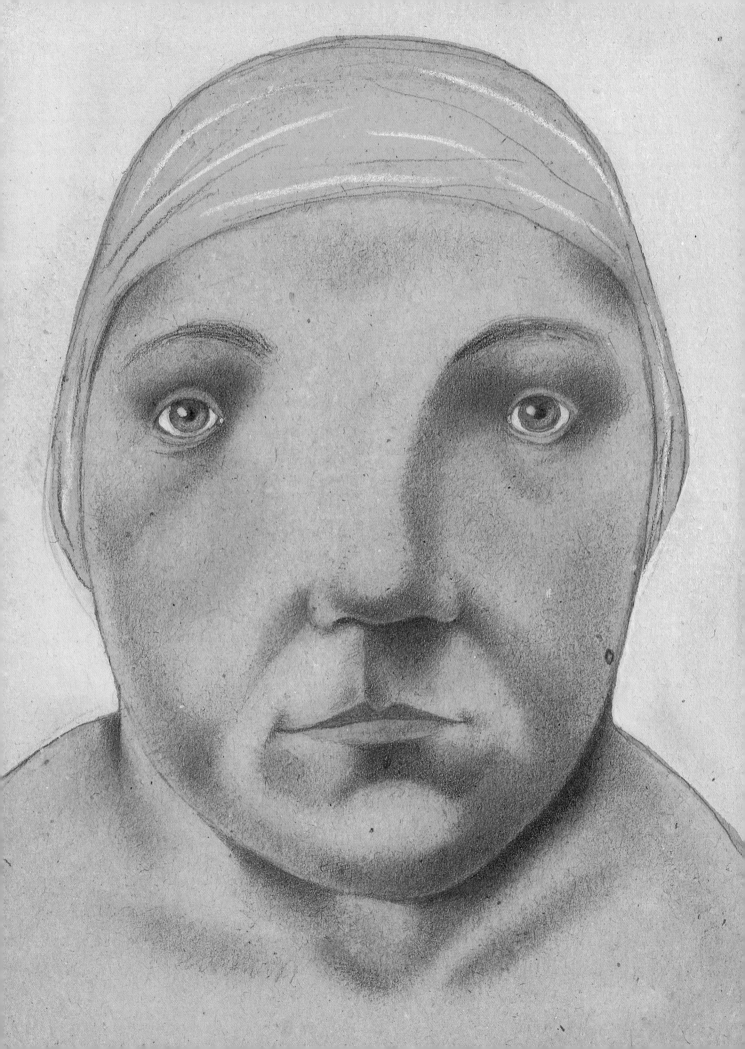

IF I had never felt pain, nobody could explain

to me what pain was.

Pain can't be compared to anything.

If I had never tasted strawberries,

somebody could still more or less explain

what strawberries taste like. Kind of

in between cherries and apples.

Nothing comes close to pain.

Not even sorrow.

But everyone knows what pain is. Me, too.

The pain of a throbbing finger. Toothache.

Headache. Stomachache. Earache. The pain

of a broken leg, blood under a nail.

There is more pain in the world than anything.

PAULA

I WISH I had an extremely unusual pet.

A pet that nobody else has.

Something like a rhinoceros.

I think I'd call him Ryan. Ryan the rhinoceros.

Late in the afternoon my mother would ask,

"Do you want to take Ryan out for a walk?"

Then we'd go to the public gardens behind our house.

Ryan and me.

People would stare.

"Is that your rhino?"

"Can we pet him?"

"Sure."

They would carefully stroke his back.

And if I was tired, I'd sit on his back with my arms

around his neck and then we'd trot home.

At night he'd stand next to my bed.

I'd hang my jeans on his horn.

He wouldn't mind at all.

RAFE

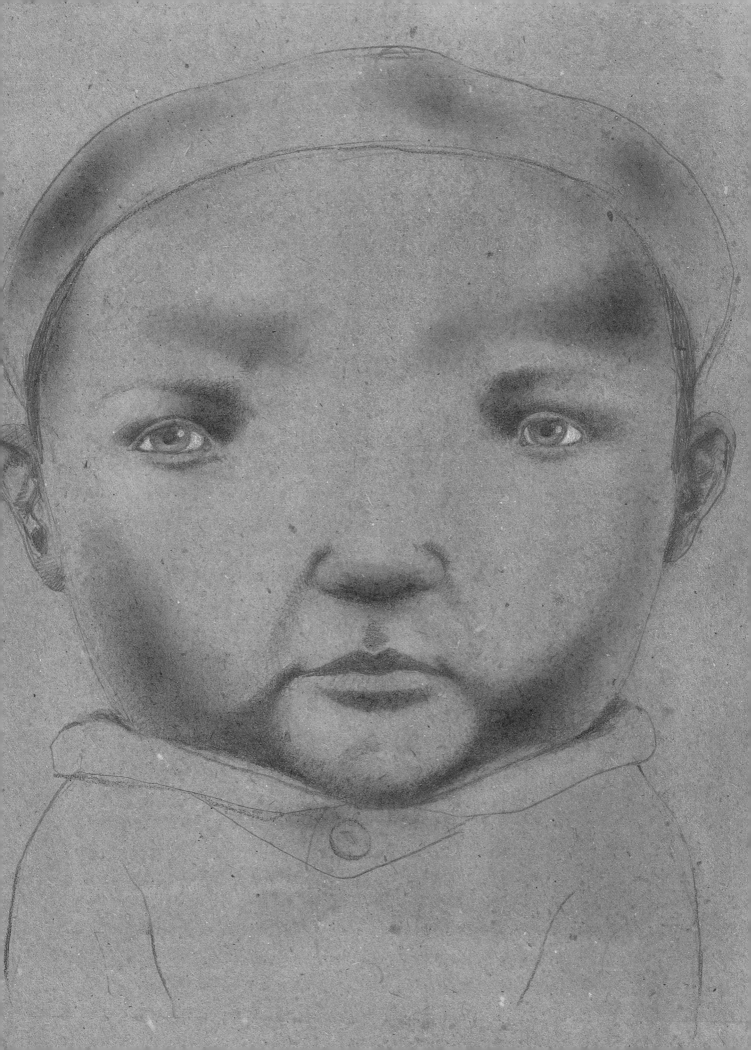

I wish

I wish

I could trust myself, that I knew I was someone I could

count on, someone I could share my secrets with.

I'd wake myself up in the middle of the night

and want to tell myself all the things

I didn't know yet, all my secrets.

But I don't trust myself.

I let myself sleep.

It's cold.

I lay an extra blanket over myself.

I'm still in the dark.

I WANT to fight something,

but I still have to decide what.

Not injustice, anyway.

Everybody's already fighting that.

I want to fight something

nobody else is fighting.

Vanity, maybe.

Or tickling.

I really hate tickling.

I WISH I was a little cuter, nicer, friendlier,

funnier, happier, snappier, braver, brighter,

brainier, more exciting and more unusual

than I am now and someone told me:

"No way, like you were before, that was just perfect."

And I am! I know it!

BERTHA

I WISH I was standing at a crossroads

      and there were two empty roads in front of me.

      But if I stop to think about it, I am always

      standing at a crossroads and there are always

      two empty roads in front of me, and maybe even

      three or four roads, straight roads, windy roads,

      roads lined with poplars, roadsides full of daisies

      and dandelions and stinging nettles and barbed wire.

      I can't choose because I don't know where

      any of those roads go.

      Nobody knows, I think to comfort myself.

      And then I walk on along one of those roads,

      it doesn't matter which, going somewhere.

IRMA

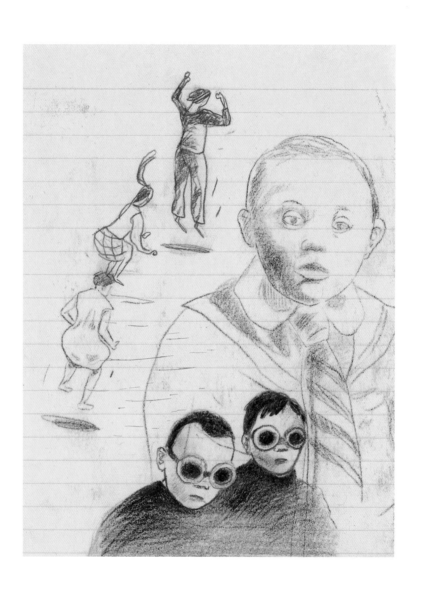

I WISH there was a way back and I stopped

while everyone else carried on.

"Aren't you coming?"

"No, I'm going back."

"That's impossible!"

But it would be possible and I'd go back, alone,

past yesterday and the day before yesterday

and last week and last month, last year.

I know exactly where I'd go back to.

And when I got there, I'd look around and

recognize everything and take a different path,

one with a bend in it and a gutter alongside it, not a ditch.

Then I'd come back out at today,

but nothing would be the same.

"There's only one way," everyone says. "This way."

Pointing ahead.

I don't say a word.

ALEX

I WISH I was unappreciated, that people overlooked me,
      shrugged, walked past me without a second glance,
      blew me off their hand like a fruit fly, flicked
      me out of a glass of lemonade with the point of a knife
      like a wasp, had almost completely forgotten me,
      and that I then suddenly, one morning,
      to everyone's surprise...

      (I still have to think what)

I WISH I knew what life is.

    Maybe it's a single straw I'm clutching at,

    just like everyone, while thinking, just like everyone,

    that life is a vast field with thousands of stalks

    swaying in the wind, with poppies and cornflowers

    blooming here and there between them,

    under an immense sky

    with the sun shining down while clouds bunch together,

    then dissolve again.

    But it's a square inch in fading light

    with just one solitary straw.

    I'm going to hang on tight.

VIOLETTA

I would

I would

save the world if I needed to.

If someone came up to me and asked,

"Could you save the world?"

"When?"

"Now."

"Now?"

"Yes, now, right away. Not a second to lose!"

I wouldn't hesitate for a moment, but save the world,

even before I asked how: there wouldn't be time

for that. I can only hope it won't be too complicated.

Otherwise I won't manage and the world will be lost.

I WISH there was something I could stop doing,

    that I could call it a day.

    I don't know what it might be, but there

    has to be something.

    One day I'll realize,

    it's time to call it a day!

    The sun will be shining, the trees in blossom,

    the birds singing.

    I'll slow down, wait for a moment,

    give a friendly nod and say, "So..."

    Then I'll call it a day.

    A perfect day.

    After that I'll never have to wish for anything

    ever again and it will always stay April,

    early April.